W9-AFY-929

The Donkey's Christmas Song

written and illustrated by

NANCY TAFURI

With Peace and Joy! Nancy Tafuri

DUCK POND PRESS • CONNECTICUT

Hee-Aw!.....

Copyright © 2002 by Nancy Tafuri. All rights reserved.

Originally published by Scholastic Press. Now published by Duck Pond Press. Publishers since 2005.
Duck Pond Press and its logo are a registered trademark. No part of this publication may be reproduced,
or stored in a retrieval system, or transmitted in any form or by any means, electronic,
mechanical, photocopying, recording, or otherwise without written permission of the publisher.
For information regarding permissions, write to Duck Pond Press,
Attention Permissions Department, PO Box 168, Roxbury, Ct. 06783

Library of Congress Cataloging-in-Publication Data. Tafuri, Nancy
The Donkey's Christmas Song / by Nancy Tafuri.— p.cm.
Summary: Various animals welcome a new baby born in a stable with their special
sounds, but the donkey is afraid that his braying will be to harsh.
ISBN 978-0-9763369-5-2

[1.Animals—Fiction 2.Jesus Christ—Nativity—Fiction 3.Christmas—Fiction.4.] I.Title

The illustrations for this book were created using watercolors, pencils and ink.
The text is set in 36-pt Calligraph 421
Title type and authors name were hand-lettered by David Coulson.
Book design by Nancy Tafuri and David Saylor

Printed in Malaysia
Duck Pond Press first edition published 2014
3 4 5 6 7 8 9 10

To Cristina
and to all
a song of peace

Under a bright star,
a long, long time ago…

a baby was born
in a stable.

The animals wanted to
welcome the baby
with their song.

But the shy little donkey
was afraid his bray
was too loud.

So, the first to welcome the baby
were the doves.
Cooo, cooo,
they sang their slow, sweet song.

Then the cow
welcomed the baby.
Mooo, mooo,
she sang her low, warm song.

Then the goats
welcomed the baby.
Maaa, maaa,
they sang their gentle song.

Then the sheep
welcomed the baby.
Baaa, baaa,
they sang their tender song.

And the chicks
welcomed the baby.
Cheep, cheep,
they sang their little song.

And the mice
welcomed the baby.
Eeep, eeep,
they sang their quiet song.

Then the baby looked over
at the shy little donkey.
The baby welcomed the donkey
with his smile.

The donkey sang his noisy song.
Hee-aw! Hee-aw! Hee-aw! . . .

and the baby laughed with joy!

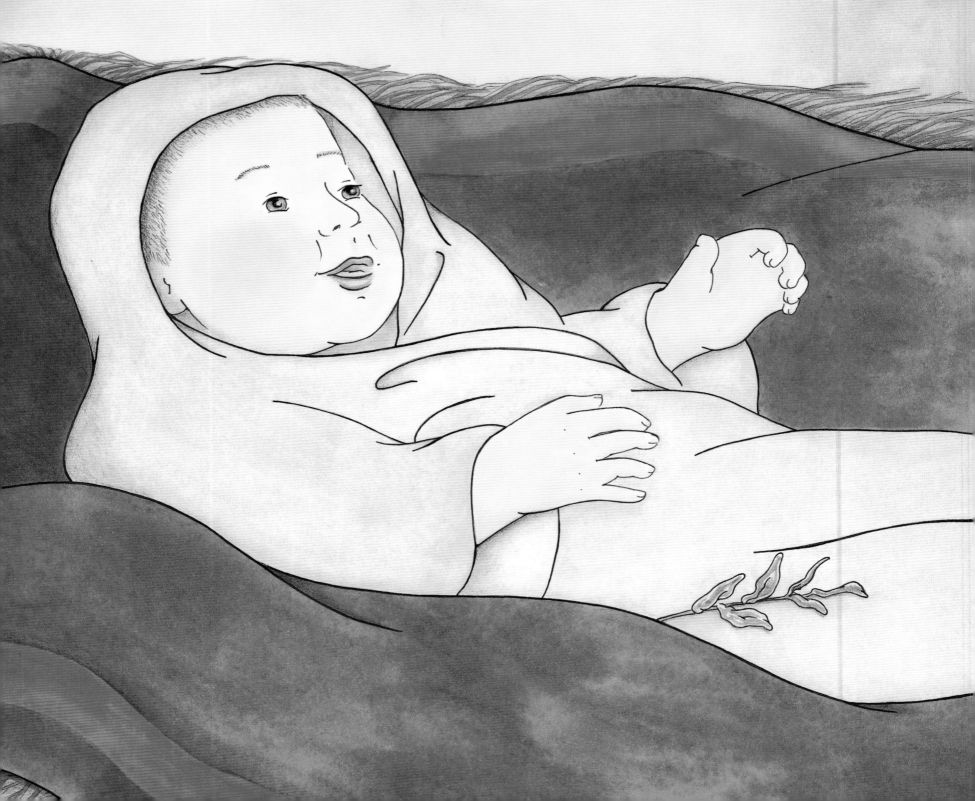

Then the donkey snuggled close. . .

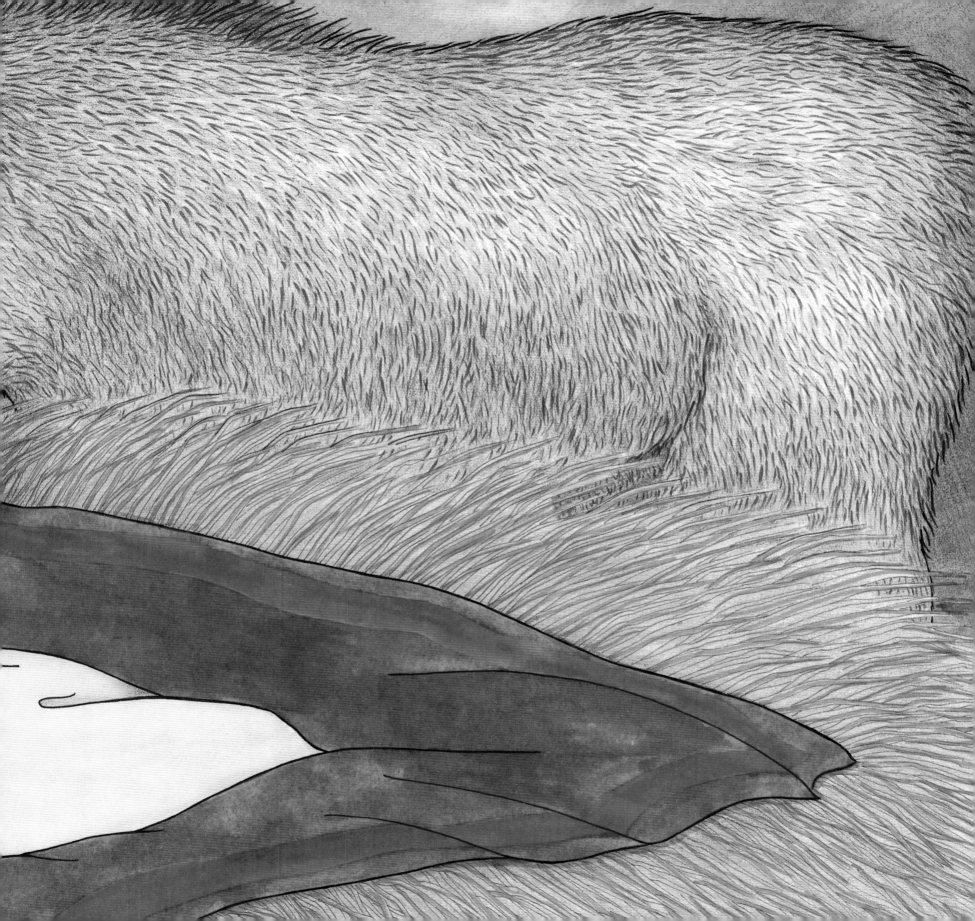

and kept the baby warm. . .

under that bright star
a long, long time ago.